🌹 A GOLDEN BOOK • NEW YORK

This special edition was printed for Kohl's Department Stores, Inc.
(for distribution on behalf of Kohl's Cares, LLC, its wholly owned subsidiary)
by Random House Children's Books, a division of Penguin Random House LLC, New York.

KOHL'S
Style 97611
Factory Number 126509
Production Date 01/2017

Ages 3 and up

MANUFACTURED IN CHINA
10 9 8 7 6 5 4 3 2 1

THE SHY
LITTLE KITTEN

by CATHLEEN SCHURR • illustrated by GUSTAF TENGGREN

Way up in the hayloft of an old red barn
lived a mother cat and her new baby kittens.
There were five bold and frisky little roly-poly
black and white kittens, and *one* little striped
kitten who was very, very shy.

One day, the five bold little roly-poly black
and white kittens and the one little roly-poly
striped kitten who was very, very shy all sat
down and washed their faces and paws with

busy little red tongues. They smoothed down
their soft baby fur and stroked their whiskers
and followed their mother down the ladder
from the hayloft—jump, jump, jump!

Then off they marched, straight out of the cool, dark barn, into the warm sunshine. How soft the grass felt under their paws! The five bold and frisky little kittens rolled over in the grass and kicked up their heels with joy.

But the shy little striped kitten just stood
off by herself at the very end of the line.

That was how she happened to see the earth
push up in a little mound right in front of her.
Then—*pop!*—up came a pointed little nose.
The nose belonged to a chubby mole.

"Good morning!" said the mole, as friendly as you please. "Won't you come for a walk with me?"

"Oh," said the shy little kitten. She looked shyly over her shoulder.

But the mother cat and her five bold and frisky kittens had disappeared from sight.

So the shy little kitten went walking with the chubby mole. Soon they met a speckled frog sitting near the pond.

"My, what big eyes he has!" whispered the shy little kitten. But the frog had sharp ears, too.

He chuckled. "My mouth is much bigger. Look!" And the frog opened his great cave of a mouth.

The mole and the kitten laughed and laughed until their sides ached.

When the kitten stopped laughing and looked around, the frog had vanished. On the pond, ripples spread out in great silver circles.

"I really should be getting back to my mother and the others," said the shy little kitten, "but I don't know where to find them."

"I'll show you," said a strange voice. And out of the bushes bounded a shaggy black puppy.

"Oh, thank you," said the shy little kitten.
"Good-bye, mole."

So off they went together, the shy kitten
and the shaggy puppy dog. The little kitten,
of course, kept her eyes shyly on the ground.

But the shaggy puppy stopped to bark,
"Woof, woof," at a red squirrel in a tree. He
was full of mischief.

"Chee, chee, chee," the squirrel chattered
back. And she dropped a hickory nut right
on the puppy's nose. She was very brave.

"Wow, wow, wow," barked the mischievous
puppy, and off they went toward the farm.
Soon they came bounding out of the woods,
and there before them stretched the farmyard.

"Here we are," said the shaggy puppy dog.
So down the hillside they raced, across the
bridge above the brook, and straight on into
the farmyard.

In the middle of the farmyard was the mother cat with her five bold and frisky little black and white kittens. In a flash, the mother cat was beside her shy kitten, licking her all over with a warm red tongue.

"Where have you been?" she cried. "We're all ready to start on a picnic."

The picnic was for all the farmyard animals.
There were seeds for the chickens, water bugs
for the ducks, and carrots and cabbages for
the rabbits. There were flies for the frog, and
there was a trough of mash for the pig.

Yum, yum, yum! How good it all was!

After they had finished eating, everyone was just beginning to feel comfortable and drowsy, when suddenly the frog jumped straight into the air, eyes almost popping out of his head.

"Help! Run!" he cried.

The frog made a leap for the brook.

Everyone scrambled after him and tumbled into the water.

"What is it?" asked the shy little kitten.

"A bee!" groaned the frog. "I bit a bee!"

Then they saw that one side of his mouth was puffed up like a green balloon.

Everybody laughed. They couldn't help
it. Even the frog laughed. They all looked so
funny as they climbed out of the brook.

The shy little kitten stood off to one side. She felt so good that she turned a backward somersault, right there in the long meadow grass. "This is the best day ever," said the shy little kitten.

The Little
RED HEN

illustrated by J. P. MILLER

One summer day the Little Red Hen found a grain of wheat.

"A grain of wheat!" said the Little Red Hen to herself. "I will plant it."

She asked the duck:
"Will you help me plant this grain of wheat?"
"Not I!" said the duck.

She asked the goose:
"Will you help me plant this grain of wheat?"
"Not I!" said the goose.

She asked the cat:
"Will you help me plant this grain of wheat?"
"Not I!" said the cat.

She asked the pig:
"Will you help me plant this grain of wheat?"
"Not I!" said the pig.

"Then I will plant it myself," said
the Little Red Hen. And she did.

Soon the wheat grew tall, and the Little Red Hen
knew it was time to reap it.
"Who will help me reap the wheat?" she asked.

"Not I!" said the duck.

"Not I!" said the goose.

"Not I!" said the cat.

"Not I!" said the pig.

"Then I will reap it myself,"
said the Little Red Hen.
And she did.

She reaped the wheat, and it was ready to be taken to the mill and made into flour.

"Who will help me carry the wheat to the mill?" she asked.

"Not I!" said the duck.
"Not I!" said the goose.
"Not I!" said the cat.
"Not I!" said the pig.

"Then I will carry it myself," said the Little
Red Hen. And she did. She carried the wheat
to the mill, and the miller made it into flour.

When she got it home, she asked, "Who will help
me make the flour into dough?"
"Not I!" said the duck.
"Not I!" said the goose.
"Not I!" said the cat.
"Not I!" said the pig.

"Then I will make the dough myself," said the Little Red Hen. And she did.

Soon the bread was ready to go into the oven.

"Who will help me bake the bread?" said the Little Red Hen.

"Not I!" said the duck.

"Not I!" said the goose.

"Not I!" said the cat.

"Not I!" said the pig.

"Then I will bake it myself," said the Little
Red Hen. And she did.
  After the loaf had been taken from the
oven, it was set on the windowsill to cool.

"And now," said the Little Red Hen,
"who will help me eat the bread?"
"I will!" said the duck.

"I will!" said the goose.

"I will!" said the cat.

"I will!" said the pig.

"No, I will eat it myself!" said the Little
Red Hen. And she did.

THE LITTLE RED
Caboose

by MARIAN POTTER • illustrated by TIBOR GERGELY

The little red caboose
always came last.

First came the big black engine,
puffing and chuffing.

Then came the boxcars,

then the oil cars,

then the coal cars,

then the flat cars.
Sometimes they were
switched around in different ways.

But the little red caboose
always came last.

Boys and girls waved
at the big black engine.

They listened to the boxcars
and the oil cars
and the coal cars
and the flat cars
go *clickety clack.*

But by the time the little red
caboose came along, the boys and girls
were turning away.

   Because the little red caboose
always came last.

"Oh, smoke!" said the little red caboose.
"I wish I were a flat car
or a coal car or an oil car
or a boxcar, so boys and
girls would wave at me.

"How I wish I were a big black engine,
puffing and chuffing way up
at the front of the train!

"But I'm just the little old red caboose.
Nobody cares for me."

One day the train
started up a mountain.
Up went the big black engine.
Up went the boxcars.
Up went the oil cars.

Up went the coal cars.
Up went the flat cars.
Up went the little red caboose.

"Hang on tight, little caboose,"
called the flat car.
    "This is a long tall mountain.
And you are the last car
on the train."
    "Don't I know it!"
sighed the little red caboose.
"Poor me!"

The train went slower
and slower and s-l-o-w-e-r.
Soon it was hardly moving.
It looked as if that train
could not get up the mountain.

"Look out, little caboose!"
called the flat car.
 "The train is starting to slip
back down this long tall mountain!"
 "Not if I can help it!"
said the little red caboose.

And he slammed on his brakes.
And he held tight to the tracks.
And he kept that train
from sliding down the mountain!

Then, *bump!*
The little red caboose
felt something push him
from behind.

It was two big black engines.
They pushed the train up to the top
of the mountain.

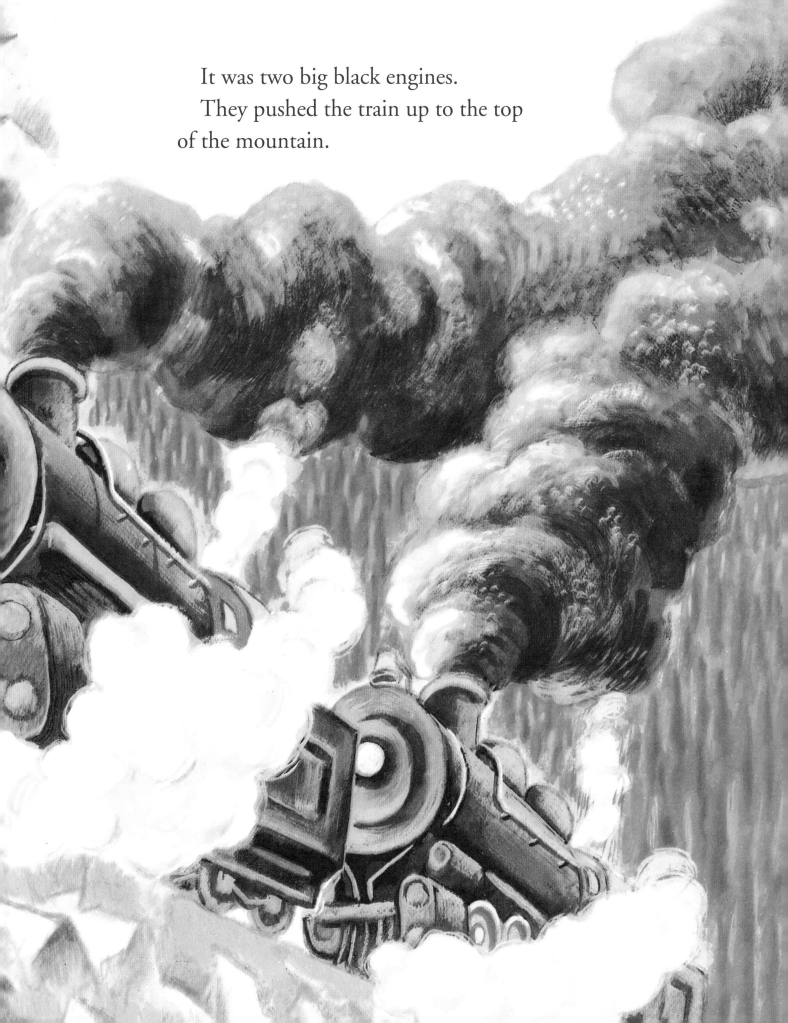

"We couldn't have done it,"
said the big black engines,
"if it had not been for the
little red caboose."
Everyone cheered.
And the little red caboose
nearly burst with pride.

Now, children wave at the big
black engine and at all the cars.

But they save their biggest waves for
the little red caboose. Because the little red
caboose saved the train.